Terror at
Troy

Secret in the Attic series
Read them all!

**Lost in the Labyrinth**

**Peril at the Pyramids**

**Panic in Pompeii**

**Terror at Troy**

# Terror at Troy

by L. A. Peacock

illustrated by Nathan Hale

**Scholastic Inc.**
New York Toronto London Auckland
Sydney Mexico City New Delhi Hong Kong

For Alexander and Eve Frois,
who love puzzles and stories, with love—*L.A.F.*



ISBN 978-0-545-34063-2



12 11 10 9 8 7 6 5 4 3 2 1 12 13 14 15 16 17/0

Printed in the U.S.A. 40

First Scholastic printing, January 2012

## Chapter 1

# Treasure in the Trunk

Josh sat on the bed, reading. It was dark outside, nearly five o'clock. Winter days were short and cold in Boston. Snow was starting to fall.

"Hey, is that a *book*?" Jess asked, peeking into the room. Her brother was always playing video games.

Her ten-year-old twin looked up.

Jess stood in the doorway, with her arms crossed. A big grin was on her face.

"Very funny," he said, and turned the page.

Josh was reading about Greek myths and legends. He loved the old stories, especially since their time travels to ancient Crete with Uncle Harry.

"Let's go," said Jess, grabbing the flashlight. She raced down the hallway.

"Again?" said Josh. He dropped the book on the bed.

Jess looked over her shoulder and frowned.

"Hurry!" she called, climbing the ladder to the attic.

"Okay, okay," he said. "I'm coming." Every day they checked the attic for clues from Uncle Harry. Weeks had passed since their last adventure.

Josh stepped into the dark attic. Jess was in the corner. The beam of the flashlight was on the old trunk, Uncle Harry's magic trunk.

Their uncle was an explorer lost in time. He left sacred objects in the trunk to keep them safe. Jess and Josh helped Uncle Harry return these treasures to their true owners.

Slowly, Jess opened the lid of the trunk. Today the trunk *wasn't* empty.

"He was here!" cried Jess with excitement.

She leaned in and pulled out Uncle Harry's brown leather journal.

"Uncle Harry's bag is here, too," said Jess.

Josh rushed over and grabbed the leather bag. He reached in and pulled out something shiny.

"It's here," said Josh. He gazed at the round metal device in his hand. It looked like a clock. Two hands set the time. A third hand set the direction: N, S, E, and W. The mysterious time-compass had taken the twins to ancient Egypt and to the Roman city of Pompeii.

Josh looked closely at the time-compass. The hands were locked into place. Uncle Harry had set the device to a new place and time. It was ready to take them on a new adventure. *But where?* he wondered.

"Anything else in the bag?" asked Jess.

Josh reached in. Something was at the bottom.

"This stuff is heavy!" he said. Josh scooped

up a bunch of old gold jewelry.

"Let me see," said Jess, handing the flashlight to Josh. She spread out the pieces on the attic floor. There were fancy earrings, some bracelets, necklaces, and more.

Jess picked up something. It looked like a hat, only made of gold.

"Wow," she said. "This is pretty." The gold sparkled in the beam of the flashlight.

"Where did Uncle Harry get this stuff?" asked Josh.

"I don't know," said Jess. "Check his journal."

Josh handed the flashlight to Jess and picked up the brown leather book. The pages were filled with their uncle's notes from his travels. Josh flipped to the last entry and pointed to a map.

Jess moved in closer.

"Okay, there's the map of ancient Greece and Troy," said Jess, "and the wooden horse."

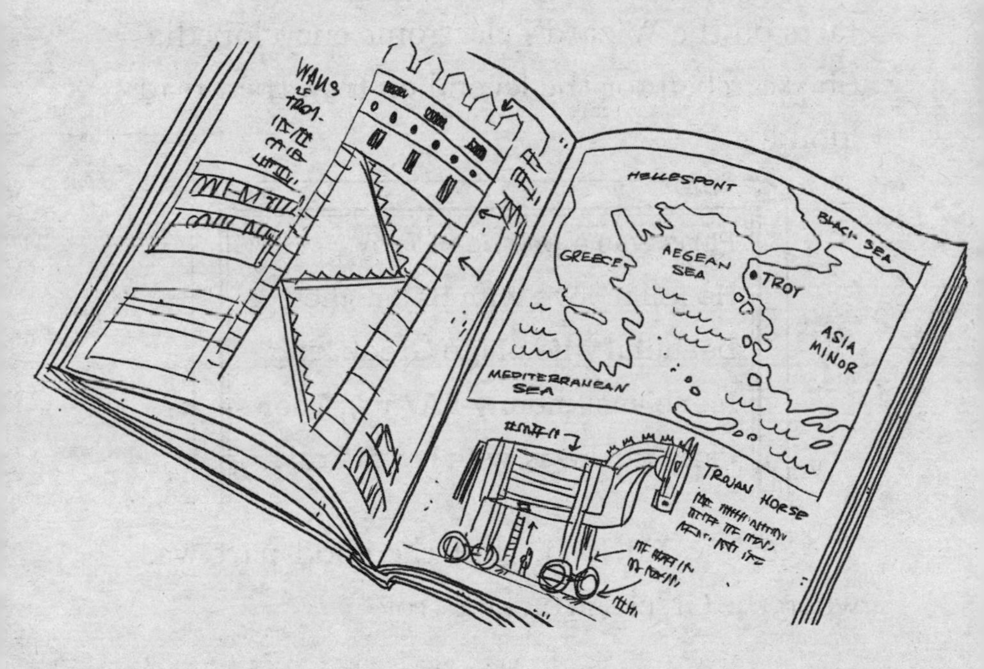

"The Trojan War," said Josh. "I've been reading about the legend. The Greeks tricked the Trojans. Soldiers hid inside a huge wooden horse. Then they climbed out and attacked when the Trojans were asleep."

"Maybe there's a clue in that old story," said Jess.

She reached into her pocket and turned on the Book Wizard. Jess looked up all kinds of facts on the Wizard's electronic encyclopedia. She searched for the legend of Troy, then read aloud:

wizard

**Paris was a prince of Troy. He fell in love with Helen, the beautiful wife of the Greek king Menelaus (menny-LAY-us). Then Paris ran away with her to Troy.**

"Yeah," said Josh, "but the good part was when the Greeks attacked Troy."

Jess clicked again.

o wizard

**The Greeks surrounded Troy for ten years. They tried to rescue Helen. Menelaus got help from Achilles (a-KILL-ees) and Odysseus (o-DEE-si-us). They were great soldiers and Greek heroes.**

"Any more clues in the journal?" asked Josh. "We still don't know about the gold jewelry."

Jess turned the page. "What's that?" she asked.

"Looks like a secret code," said Josh. The Greeks were famous for their number tricks.

They stared at the puzzle. Numbers ran down and across the sides. Letters of the alphabet filled the boxes.

"Uncle Harry left us a message," said Josh. "In secret code."

"Look at those pairs of numbers on the side," said Jess. "Each letter has a pair of numbers."

She pointed to the numbers "32" and "51" and the letters "H" and "E."

Josh moved his fingers up and down the puzzle.

"I've got it!" he cried out. "The first number in the pair is for the row, going across. The second number is for the column, going up and down. Where the numbers cross the grid is the secret letter."

"So," said Jess, "the pair '13' must be an 'L.'"

"And another 'E' for '51,'" said Josh, "and 'N' for '33.'"

"HELEN!" they said together.

"Cool," said Josh. He was sure now. Their uncle was sending them to Troy.

Jess typed some words into the Wizard and clicked. She wanted to find out more about Troy and Helen.

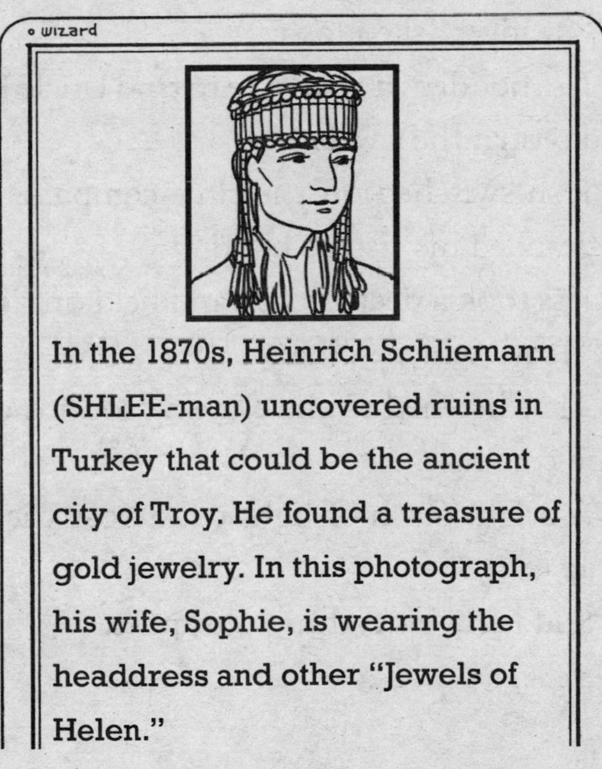


In the 1870s, Heinrich Schliemann (SHLEE-man) uncovered ruins in Turkey that could be the ancient city of Troy. He found a treasure of gold jewelry. In this photograph, his wife, Sophie, is wearing the headdress and other "Jewels of Helen."

Jess turned the screen toward Josh. "Those jewels belonged to Helen," she said in a quiet voice.

Josh smiled to himself. He gathered the jewels and Uncle Harry's journal. Then he tossed them into the leather bag.

Jess stood up. She tucked the Wizard into her pocket.

"Ready?" asked Josh.

Jess nodded. It was time to find Uncle Harry and return the jewels.

Josh switched on the time-compass. Then he grabbed his sister's hand.

Jess took a deep breath and held on tightly.

"Troy," whispered Josh.

They listened to the clicking sounds of the time-compass.

A bright flash of light cut across the dark attic.

Suddenly, everything was quiet.

Chapter 2

# On the Beach

Jess opened her eyes. She was sitting on a wooden bench.

"Oops!" cried Jess. She fell forward.

"Hey," she said. "We're on a boat!" The bench was rocking back and forth. A wave of cool water splashed over the side.

Jess wiped her face with the hem of her white dress. Her sweatshirt, jeans, and sneakers were gone. Her new clothes were magic, like the time-compass.

Josh sat up beside her. The water had hit him, too.

"Where are we?" he asked, rubbing his eyes. He was wearing a white tunic with a rope belt.

On his feet were sandals with leather straps.

"I don't know," said Jess. "But we're not moving." She looked around. "Maybe we're somewhere in ancient Greece, or Troy."

She felt in her pocket for the Wizard. It was safe.

Josh stood up and peered over the railing at the shore. Tents were set up in long rows along the beach. He could see men and horses on the practice fields.

"Soldiers," said Josh, pointing to the army camp. "Hundreds of them."

"Sit down," shouted Jess, pulling hard on her brother's tunic. "Don't let them see us."

Josh groaned. Jess liked to give orders.

Behind the bench were stacks of helmets, shields, and swords.

"Oh, boy," said Josh. He crawled over to the weapons and grabbed a sword.

"Hey," said Jess. "Put that down." Josh was holding a shield and swinging the sword wildly. He had put on a leather vest and a helmet with a red crest on top.

"Oh, man," said Josh. "This is great. Do I look like a soldier?"

Jess stared at her brother. He was leaping across the deck with his sword.

"Are you nuts?" she said. "Stop playing games. We need a plan."

Josh looked around. More boats were anchored next to theirs. Rows of oars ran along the sides of each boat. Wooden rams covered with metal stuck out at the front. At top speed, the rams could punch holes in enemy ships.

"Cool," said Josh. "We're on a Greek battleship." He remembered the legend of the Trojan War. King Menelaus had gathered a fleet of a thousand ships filled with Greek soldiers. Then they sailed to Troy to rescue Helen.

"There's a war going on," said Jess. "Aren't you worried about finding Uncle Harry?"

"Maybe he's with the Greeks and King Menelaus," said Josh. He watched the soldiers on the beach practicing with their swords.

"Or with the Trojans," said Jess. Uncle Harry's leather bag was on Josh's shoulder. The Jewels of Helen were inside.

Jess peered over the side. Waves were breaking along the shore. "First we have to get off this boat."

"We're not far from land," Josh said. He looked down. "The water doesn't look very deep."

Josh started to jump over the side.

"Wait," yelled Jess. "I have an idea."

Jess ran over to the shields. They were made of animal skins stretched across wooden frames. She lifted one above her head.

"These aren't heavy," said Jess. Suddenly, she took the shields, rushed to the side, and tossed them into the water. One shield touched the next one.

"Hey," said Josh, shaking his head, "are you crazy?"

"Look," said Jess, grinning. "It's a bridge!"

Josh glanced at the floating shields. They made a line to the shore.

"Go," said Jess, pointing to the bridge of shields.

"Okay," said Josh. He jumped over the railing and landed on the first shield. He leaped across the shields to the sandy beach.

It was Jess's turn. "Come on!" yelled Josh, over his shoulder. "And bring a sword." They needed to look like soldiers, too.

Jess reached for a sword. Then she stepped over the side and skipped across the shields.

"Grab my hand," said Josh. He took the sword and pulled Jess onto dry land.

Josh slipped the sword through his belt.

"Let's go," said Jess, picking up two wet shields. "That way," she said, pointing.

A big white tent was just ahead.

## Chapter 3

# The Army Camp

Josh and Jess walked over the hot sand toward the big tent.

Some men were sharpening metal swords and spears. Others were repairing holes in the leather shields. The women nearby were adding wood to the fires and filling clay cooking pots with water. Baskets were piled high with fish, fruit, and vegetables.

"Keep your head down," whispered Josh. "Maybe nobody will notice us."

Jess followed a few steps behind Josh. They got closer.

"Whoops!" cried Jess. Her sandal caught on a rock. Josh caught her before she fell.

A man with a long scar on his face looked up. He frowned at Jess.

"Put those shields over here," said the man, pointing to a place at his feet. Jess nodded and dropped the shields. Like magic, she understood the ancient Greek language.

Josh looked around. A servant girl near the fire was watching them. She was young, about fifteen. Her hair was dark brown. It was long and curly.

Josh sighed. The girl was beautiful.

She called to him. Her voice was soft and musical.

"Do you mean me?" asked Josh. He could understand and speak the strange language, too.

The girl smiled and waved Josh over. He rushed to her side.

"Can you help me?" she asked, pointing to a pile of wood.

Josh nodded. He grabbed some logs and

carried them over to the cooking fire.

"My name is Josh," he said, placing a big log on the fire. "This is my sister, Jess." They sat down near the fire.

"I am called Briseis," she said. She was beating a small octopus with a rock. Then she threw the octopus into the cooking pot.

Briseis pushed a basket in front of Jess. She handed her the rock. "Beat these for me," she said, "until they are tender."

She got up to get more water.

Jess stared at the rock. "Gross," she said, holding her nose. The octopuses were alive and squiggling in the basket. Jess put the rock aside. She took the Wizard from her pocket and typed. On the screen she read:

Wizard

Briseis (briss-EH-iss) is a princess of Troy. She was captured by the Greeks and became Achilles' servant girl.

Jess showed the screen to Josh.

"Wow," said Josh. "Achilles is a Greek hero. Their best fighter."

Jess thought about Briseis. *A royal princess, now a slave. Maybe she would help them?*

Suddenly, rumbling sounds came from the practice field behind the tent.

"There!" cried Jess, pointing. A chariot with two horses pulled up next to Briseis. "That could be him."

Josh stared at the driver of the chariot. He was tall and strong. Over his red tunic, he wore leather armor with metal plates. Thick muscles ran along his bare arms and legs. A bronze helmet covered his head.

"Achilles," whispered Josh. "He's immortal, like a god. That's what the Greek myths say."

Jess searched the Wizard. She read aloud:

o wizard

**The ancient Greeks believed that Achilles' mother was a goddess. She gave him special powers. When he was a baby, she held him by his tiny heel and dipped him into a magical river. Her son would then live forever.**

Suddenly, a horn sounded in the distance.

"What's going on?" said Josh, looking all around. Some soldiers were rushing out of tents with swords. Others were climbing into chariots with weapons.

"I don't know," said Jess. She was frightened. Everyone was shouting.

Just then, Briseis stood on her toes and said something to Achilles. She turned and pointed to Jess and Josh. Briseis jumped into the chariot as Achilles steered the horses toward the big tent.

"Oh, man," said Josh, running toward the chariot. The horses were excited, kicking up sand. Achilles held the reins tightly, keeping the cart steady.

"Come," said Briseis, waving to Josh. "Ride with Achilles and carry his shield and javelin." She ran to the tent and handed Josh a long spear and shield.

Josh tossed the shield to Achilles and jumped into the chariot. Flipping the shield

to his back, Achilles shook the reins. Josh held the javelin upright. His other hand gripped the side of the cart.

Achilles' chariot sped away in a cloud of dust. The other soldiers in chariots took off after Achilles. Behind them, more soldiers formed into lines and marched over the sand.

"Where are they going?" yelled Jess. It was hard to hear with all the noise around them.

Briseis looked worried.

"Troy," she said. "To battle with my cousins. Hector and Paris."

Jess gasped. She watched the Greek army disappear over the sand dunes.

*Josh*, she thought. *What trouble are you in now?*

## Chapter 4

# The Battle for Troy

The chariot raced across the hard sand.

Josh hung on as the wheels bumped along the road. They passed fields planted with cotton, sunflowers, and wheat. Cattle and horses grazed on the grassy plains.

Up ahead on a high hill, Josh saw the city.

"Troy," he said to himself. Thick stone walls protected the city. Tall towers at the corners rose above the sloping walls.

Achilles pointed to the highest tower at the main gate. "That's the Watchtower."

Josh nodded. He stared at the Trojan soldiers in the tower windows. They held bows with arrows aimed at the Greek soldiers below. More Trojan soldiers with weapons stood on top of the city walls.

Achilles pulled up in front of the big gate. A thick wooden log held the heavy doors shut. The Trojans were safe inside.

King Priam with his sons Paris and Hector watched from the tower. The Greek army came closer and closer. The old Trojan king gazed across the battlefield at his enemy.

The Greek chariots lined up behind Achilles. They waited for the soldiers marching by foot. When they arrived an hour later, the soldiers formed in rows. Thousands of Greek soldiers drew their swords. They were ready for battle.

A strange quiet filled the air.

Suddenly, a tall Trojan soldier stood on the Watchtower. His blue-crested helmet and silver armor marked him as a prince of Troy. He waved his long sword above his head.

"Who's that?" asked Josh.

"Hector," mumbled Achilles. "Son of King Priam. Troy's best fighter."

"Achilles!" shouted Hector in a loud voice. "Prepare to die!" Then the tall Trojan turned and left the tower.

Achilles steered the chariot behind the Greek lines.

"Wait here," he said, handing the reins to Josh. Achilles leaped from the chariot with his sword held high. The Greek soldiers moved aside. Achilles ran toward the gate to meet his enemy.

The huge city gates of Troy opened. Hector stepped out. He held his sword in front of him. His shield was in his other hand. The Trojan prince stood in the middle of the open space, waiting.

A single soldier burst through the Greek lines.

Achilles rushed at Hector, aiming his sword at Hector's chest.

The Greek soldiers roared for Achilles. Up on the wall, the Trojans cheered for Hector. The sounds of clashing swords filled the air.

Josh stood in the chariot. He couldn't see the fight. All around him, the Greek soldiers were stomping their feet. They yelled loudly. Then there was silence.

Suddenly, a soldier stepped into the chariot and pushed Josh aside.

"What happened?" asked Josh, jumping into another chariot.

The soldier grabbed the reins. "Achilles won the fight!" he shouted as he wheeled the chariot around. "Hector is dead."

The chariot raced toward the city walls. Achilles knelt next to the body on the ground. With leather straps, he tied Hector's body to the back of his chariot.

Achilles stepped into the chariot and shook the reins. King Priam watched in horror. The Greek hero raced away from Troy with his son's body.

# Chapter 5

# A Hero's Funeral

Jess and Briseis gazed across the sandy beach. They watched for hours, waiting for the Greek soldiers to return from Troy.

Briseis spoke first. "There," she cried. "Up ahead." There was a big cloud of dust rising in the distance. Chariots.

"Let's go!" yelled Jess. She was worried about Josh.

They ran to the edge of the camp. Jess moved aside as the chariots raced by. Achilles rode alone. He steered the horses to his tent. Briseis rushed to him.

"Jess! Jess!" called a familiar voice. Jess turned. Josh was racing toward her.

"Are you okay?" she cried as she pulled her brother behind some wooden barrels. Josh nodded, falling to the ground. He was out of breath.

"I saw it," he said with excitement. "Troy! The walls were so high. There were soldiers in the big tower. King Priam and his sons, too."

"Did you see Uncle Harry?" asked Jess. "Was Helen there, too?"

Josh shook his head.

"No," he said. "But there was a fight, and Hector was killed. Achilles brought his body back to camp."

Jess reached into her pocket and pulled out the Wizard. She wanted to know more about King Priam and Hector. Jess typed in some words and read aloud:

wizard

**The ancient myth says that Hermes, the messenger of the gods, came to King Priam in a**

o wizard

**dream. He told the old king to go to the Greek camp. The gods would protect him. He must beg Achilles for his son's body. Hector must have a hero's funeral.**

"What now?" asked Jess. "Will this war end soon?"

Josh sighed. "Forget it," he said. "The Trojans are safe behind their walls."

Jess nodded. She glanced at the big tent. Briseis and the servants were preparing the evening meal.

"Come on," said Jess, pointing toward the cooking fires. It was time to gather more wood.

Josh stood up. "Maybe the king will come for his son."

"Soon," said Jess. "I hope he comes soon."

Together they walked over to help Briseis.

* * *

The night was dark, but the moon was bright just before dawn. Most of the soldiers were asleep. The Greek camp was quiet.

Josh kept his eyes on the road to Troy. He saw a distant shadow in the moonlight.

"Wake up," whispered Josh. He shook his sister gently.

Jess yawned. She opened her eyes slowly.

"Do you see King Priam?" asked Jess, rubbing her eyes. Every night they waited for the Trojan king to come for his son's body.

"There," he said. Someone was coming across the sand. The horses were unusually quiet. Even the guards didn't see the enemy chariot.

"Strange," whispered Jess. "It has to be the old king. Maybe the gods are leading him here."

"Yeah," said Josh. "Just like the myth says. He's coming for Hector's body."

Josh and Jess moved closer to the big tent and crouched behind the wooden barrels. The chariot pulled to a stop. The king nodded to his driver and got out slowly. Achilles stepped out of the tent. He waved for the king to follow him back inside.

The driver of the chariot pulled back on the reins. He wore the blue tunic of a Trojan soldier. His long hair was pushed back into a ponytail. Slowly, he removed his bronze helmet.

Jess gasped. She grabbed Josh's hand and helped him up.

The driver stared at Jess and Josh. A big grin spread across his face.

"Awesome," he said, leaping from the chariot. The Trojan soldier gathered the twins into his arms.

"Uncle Harry!" they said together.

Their uncle smiled. "The time-compass brought you to me."

"You're safe!" cried Jess, hugging her uncle.

"Quick," he said, pulling away. "We haven't

much time. Do you have the jewels from the attic?"

Josh nodded. He took the leather bag from his shoulder. He reached inside and scooped out the golden jewels. Jess caught them in her dress.

"The Jewels of Helen," whispered Jess. She remembered the old photograph.

Uncle Harry held them up, one by one. The jewels sparkled in the moonlight.

Their uncle nodded. "But they belong to Troy." He stuffed the jewels into his tunic and stood up.

"Can we go with you?" asked Jess.

"No," said their uncle. "It's too dangerous."

"We can help," pleaded Josh. He wanted to see Troy again.

Uncle Harry shook his head. "Wait here," he said. "I'll be back in a few days. After Hector's funeral."

Josh glanced at the big tent. Achilles was coming out with the old king.

"Hide," said their uncle. He pushed the twins behind the wooden barrels. Then he rushed over to King Priam.

Uncle Harry carried Hector's body to the chariot. Achilles watched, his arms across his chest. Ten years of war. Everyone was tired of fighting.

Jess and Josh peeked over the barrels. The king stood next to his son's body. The chariot pushed forward and headed toward Troy.

In a cloud of dust, Uncle Harry disappeared in the early morning light.

## Chapter 6

# The Trick

"It's been a long time," said Jess. She gazed straight ahead.

"Two weeks," said Josh.

Uncle Harry had taken Helen's jewels to Troy. Jess was afraid for her uncle. "Maybe the Trojans think he's a thief."

"Don't worry," said Josh, sitting next to Jess on the hard sand. "He won't get caught."

"When he returns the jewels, we can go home," said Jess in a quiet voice.

She looked around the Greek camp. All she could see were soldiers. Every day they marched to Troy for battle. The walls of the city were too high. The Greeks could not win the war without a plan.

Some soldiers were in a circle around Achilles and Odysseus. They were kneeling on the sand, talking.

Josh whirled around as someone called his name.

"Figs," said Briseis. She held a basket in front of Josh and smiled.

"Thanks," said Josh, grabbing one of the juicy fruits. He tossed a fig to Jess.

Jess rolled the green fig in her hand, then took a bite. "Great," said Jess in surprise. She wiped the juice from her chin.

Briseis nodded. She was a good friend.

Suddenly, Odysseus grabbed a stick. He started to draw something. All eyes were on the lines in the sand.

"Odysseus is clever," said Briseis, pointing to the man with the stick. "He's the best general. But Achilles is the bravest fighter."

Now the soldiers were talking excitedly. Some were arguing loudly. Others were nodding their heads in agreement.

"What are they doing?" asked Jess.

"I don't know," said Josh, standing up. "Let's find out." With both hands, he grabbed Briseis and Jess. Together they ran over to get a better look.

They made their way just outside the circle. More soldiers had joined the crowd.

"Now what?" said Josh. He couldn't see the drawing in the sand. The men were too tall.

Jess took a deep breath. "Follow me!" she cried, and pushed into the wall of soldiers.

Josh watched as Jess squeezed through. She found spaces between the big bodies. Briseis followed quickly. Then Josh. They found themselves on the inside edge of the circle. Achilles and Odysseus were in the center.

Suddenly, it was quiet. The soldiers behind them moved aside. A path was open. Menelaus, the Greek king, stepped into the circle.

Jess stared at the huge man. He was big and muscular. His face was covered with a bushy beard. She gasped.

The king turned and glanced at Jess. He frowned, then growled when he saw Briseis.

"That's Helen's husband," whispered Briseis, pulling Jess behind her. She didn't like Menelaus. Achilles and the king did not get along. Menelaus did not want the Trojan princess in his camp.

King Menelaus took a step toward Jess and Briseis.

Josh ran up to the king. His fists were raised. "You leave them alone," he said. He tried to sound brave.

In a flash, Achilles stood in front of Josh. With legs apart, Achilles put his hands on his sword. He was eye to eye with the king.

Everyone was quiet.

King Menelaus reared his head back and roared. It was an ugly laugh.

"Foolish children," he mumbled, shaking his head.

Achilles pulled away. He was still angry. The soldiers stepped aside for their best warrior. Briseis followed Achilles back to the tent. There would be no fight today.

Slowly, the king walked to the center of the circle and crouched down. Odysseus was waving the stick, pointing to the drawing. They spoke quietly as Odysseus explained the plan. Menelaus nodded several times. He approved.

All at once, the soldiers started to murmur. Odysseus shouted orders. There was work to be done.

"Oh, man," said Josh. Before he knew it, everyone was gone.

Jess grabbed his arm. "Come on."

They crouched over the drawing. There it was. The lines in the sand showed a huge horse, made of wood.

"That's the ladder," said Josh, "and the trapdoor." He pointed to a place in the horse's big belly.

Jess reached into her pocket and pulled out the Wizard. She typed in some key words.

o wizard

**Odysseus planned a surprise attack on Troy. The Greeks left a huge wooden horse outside the city gates. Greek soldiers hid inside. The Trojans dragged the horse into the city walls. At night, when the Trojans were asleep, the Greek soldiers climbed out of the horse for the final battle.**

She turned the screen toward Josh.

"It was Odysseus's plan," she said, "to build the wooden horse."

Josh nodded, looking around. Soldiers were gathering wood. Carpenters were cutting the planks and nailing the boards into place.

By nightfall, the horse would be finished.

## Chapter 7

# The Trojan Horse

The sun was starting to set over the choppy sea. Workers were still on the beach. They were putting away their tools.

Briseis sat down next to Jess and Josh. The shadow of a huge horse fell across the hard sand.

"Look there," she said. Briseis pointed to a small group of soldiers next to the horse. Achilles and Odysseus were gathering their best men.

"Where are they going?" asked Jess. The soldiers tied swords to their belts. Red-crested helmets were on their heads. They were dressed for battle.

"To Troy," said Briseis in a quiet voice.

"Yeah," said Josh. "In the horse." He thought about the ancient Greek legend.

A thick rope was dangling under the belly of the horse. It was attached to the trapdoor.

"Bring the ladder," shouted Achilles. Soldiers placed the ladder under the trapdoor. Achilles looked up. Then he pulled the rope.

Jess, Josh, and Briseis stared at the soldiers. They were lining up behind Odysseus.

Slowly the trapdoor opened. Odysseus took the first step up the ladder. The others followed. There were twelve of them. One by one, the soldiers disappeared into the belly of the hollow horse.

Achilles was the last soldier. He started to climb the ladder.

"Wait!" shouted Briseis. She stood and ran to Achilles.

Achilles turned and smiled. He grabbed

Briseis's hand and led her behind the horse. He wanted to say good-bye.

Jess took a deep breath. She looked at Josh.

"Let's go," she whispered. "This is our chance." Jess grabbed Josh's arm and pushed him toward the horse.

Josh slowly got to his feet. "You have to be kidding," he said, looking up. Jess was already climbing the ladder.

Josh shook his head. "You're nuts!" he mumbled.

Jess turned and frowned at her brother. "Come on," she said. "We have to warn Uncle Harry."

Josh sighed. Jess was right. They had to find their uncle. He was somewhere in Troy.

"Hurry," she said, "before Achilles sees us."

Josh glanced back. No one was around. Then he raced up the ladder.

With a few steps, Jess reached the trapdoor. Josh was right behind.

Jess peeked in. The soldiers were finding places to sit. Their backs were turned.

"Now," said Jess in a quiet voice. Together, they jumped into the belly of the horse. They were small. No one saw them.

"Are you okay?" whispered Josh. He crawled over to Jess. She was hiding behind a pile of ropes.

Jess nodded, pulling Josh down next to her.

They heard voices from outside. Achilles was arguing with someone. A man.

"Who is it?" asked Jess.

Josh leaned closer. "I'm not sure," he said.

"What's he saying?" asked Jess.

Josh shrugged. He didn't know.

The voices were getting louder.

Suddenly, it was quiet again. They heard steps on the ladder. A head appeared. It was Achilles. Another man was behind him.

It was King Menelaus.

"Oh, no," groaned Jess as the king passed

by. She ducked down quickly behind the ropes. She was afraid of this man.

The soldiers moved aside for the king. He took a seat in front. It was crowded in the horse's belly.

Achilles gave the signal. The ladder was removed. He gathered up the rope and shut the trapdoor. Then Achilles sat down with the others. It was going to be a long night.

Outside, more Greek soldiers tied ropes to the horse's wheels. They pulled. With a thud, the wooden horse jerked forward.

"We're moving," whispered Josh.

Slowly the huge horse was dragged across the hard sand. Hours later, it stood in the middle of the grassy plains.

Just outside the walls of Troy.

## Chapter 8

# The Siege of Troy

It was dawn. King Priam of Troy climbed to the top of the Watchtower.

With a heavy heart, the old king gazed over the walls of the city. He was troubled. Ten years of fighting. *This war was never going to end*, he thought.

From below, a Trojan guard called to him.

"Look," the guard shouted. He pointed to something outside the main gate.

King Priam couldn't believe his eyes. In the middle of the grassy plain stood a huge wooden horse.

"What is *that*?" he asked.

The guard shook his head. "I don't know," he said. "It looks like a wooden horse."

Just then, another guard ran up to the king. He was out of breath. "The Greek camp is empty," he said with excitement. "The soldiers have sailed away during the night."

King Priam was startled. He raised his hands to thank the gods. "Yes," said the old king. "The war is finally over."

"And the horse?" asked the guard, puzzled.

King Priam stared at the wooden horse. He scratched his chin, thinking. "This horse must be a gift from the Greeks," said the king. "To bring luck to their trip home." King Priam turned to the captain of the guards.

"Pull the horse inside the walls," ordered the old king.

Slowly, the gates opened. Trojan soldiers

ran out and attached ropes to the horse. They pulled. The men did not know about the Greek soldiers hidden inside. It took many hours to wheel the horse through the gates of Troy.

Inside the horse, Jess woke up. She started to yawn.

"Shh!" whispered Josh. He had his hand over her mouth.

"Where are we?" she asked in a sleepy voice.

"Troy," said Josh. They listened to voices from the streets.

Jess sat up. She grabbed on to the side of the horse's belly.

"We're moving again," said Josh. Cheers and cries of joy came from outside. Trojans were surrounding the horse. The war was over, they thought. They had won.

Jess reached into her pocket, pulled out the Wizard, and typed. She showed Josh the screen:

wizard

The Trojans believed that the goddess Athena protected their city. A temple to Athena stood in the city center. The Greeks wanted a safe journey home. Maybe the wooden horse was a gift to the goddess.

"Odysseus's plan is working," whispered Josh. "The Trojans think the horse is a gift from King Menelaus."

"Yeah," said Jess, wiping the sweat from her face.

It was hot and smelly inside the belly of the horse. The Greek soldiers were sitting close together. They didn't move a muscle.

From her hiding place, Jess watched the big man with the bushy beard. He gave her the creeps.

King Menelaus stared straight ahead. His hand gripped his sword tightly. The lines on his face showed anger.

*What's he thinking?* Jess wondered. *Would the king take Helen back? Or would he punish her and destroy the city?*

For the rest of the day, the Trojans pulled the wooden horse along the city streets. Happy

Trojans marched alongside. By evening, they reached the temple of Athena.

"Look," said Jess. She peeked through a crack in the horse's belly. "The Trojans are having a party."

"Do you see Uncle Harry?" asked Josh.

Jess gazed at the crowd below. There were lots of people, but no Uncle Harry.

The Trojan horse stood in front of the temple. All night long, the Trojans celebrated. Even the guards had left the walls of the city to join the feast. There was no danger, they thought. The Greeks had sailed for home.

By the early hours before dawn, the city was quiet. The Trojans were asleep. They were tired from singing and dancing all night.

Odysseus stood. He crept to the trapdoor and listened. There wasn't a sound. The Trojans were all in bed. He waved to the Greek soldiers.

"Oh, man," said Josh. "They're leaving."

Jess rubbed the sleep from her eyes.

"Good," she said. It was time to look for Uncle Harry.

Odysseus gathered the men around him.

"First, we climb out," he said quietly. "Follow me to the Watchtower. Then we unlock the city gates, give a signal, and wait."

King Menelaus spoke up. "Our soldiers sailed back to Troy during the night," he said. "They're waiting outside the gates."

"Achilles," said Odysseus, turning to his best fighter. "Go to King Priam's palace. Find Helen. We'll meet you there."

The men nodded. It was a good plan. Quietly, they lashed their swords to their belts. Their shields were slung across their backs.

Odysseus opened the trapdoor. He tossed the thick rope and slid down to the ground. Jess and Josh watched the soldiers follow him, one by one. Achilles was the last to leave the horse.

"Ready," said Josh, taking Jess's hand. They crept over to the trapdoor. Jess grabbed the rope and slid down.

"Hurry," she called up to her brother. She could see Achilles racing down the street. He was running toward the palace entrance.

"Don't worry," said Josh, sliding down the rope. He jumped to the ground next to Jess. "We'll find Uncle Harry."

Achilles was almost out of sight. He ducked into the palace.

"That way," said Jess, pointing to the closing door.

They raced toward the palace. Helen was somewhere inside with her golden jewels.

And maybe their missing uncle.

## Chapter 9

# Troy Is Burning

Josh pushed against the palace door. It opened into a long dark hall. At the end, a torch cast a shadow of a man against the stone wall. It was Achilles.

"Come on," said Josh. He raced down the passageway toward the light.

Jess closed the door behind her.

Just then, someone grabbed her arm.

Jess jumped. She started to scream.

"Shh!" said a familiar voice.

"Uncle Harry!" cried Jess. Her uncle stepped out of the shadows.

"You came in the horse," he whispered. "I watched for you all night."

Jess nodded. “It was pretty scary.”

“You were brave,” said Uncle Harry, pulling her close. “Awesome!”

She looked up. “Can we go home?” Soon the Greek soldiers would attack the city.

Uncle Harry shook his head. “Not yet,” he said. “We have to find Helen.”

Her uncle took Jess’s hand. “This way,” he said, racing down the hall after Josh.

They turned the corner and ran up the stairs to a small balcony. Below was the king’s throne room. Statues of Greek gods and goddesses lined the walls.

Josh was on the balcony, kneeling behind a stone column. He smiled when he saw his uncle.

“Over here.” Josh waved for Jess and Uncle Harry to crouch down beside him. They peeked over the railing and looked down.

Below, Achilles was holding his sword above the old king’s head. King Priam was shouting.

A beautiful woman was behind the throne. She was holding a metal jar.

"Who's that?" asked Jess, staring at the woman.

"Helen," whispered Uncle Harry. He pointed to the metal jar in her hands. "Inside are the jewels of Troy. She has to hide them. There's a secret place next to the statue of Athena."

Suddenly, a shout came from the balcony across the room. A tall soldier stood with a bow and arrow. He wore the blue-crested helmet of the Trojans. The arrow was aimed at Achilles.

"Father," the soldier called to the old king. "The Greeks have come back. They are attacking the city!"

"No!" screamed the old king. King Priam stared up at his son.

Achilles turned. He knew the man with the bow and arrow.

"Paris, you are too late," shouted Achilles to the soldier in the balcony. "We will burn Troy to the ground." Achilles put his sword on the old man's chest.

Paris raised his bow and took aim. He let the arrow fly.

Achilles looked down. He felt the arrow in his left heel. His sword dropped and fell to the floor.

Something was wrong. Achilles tried to pull out the arrow. Pain raced through his leg. Achilles grabbed his heart. Then he stumbled

and fell over. The mighty Achilles, the soldier who could not die, lay still.

"Is he dead?" asked Josh, leaning over the balcony. He remembered the myths of the Trojan War.

Uncle Harry nodded. "Stay here," he said, rushing down the stairs.

Jess grabbed the Wizard and typed in some words. She read aloud:

wizard

**Achilles' Heel**

**The arrow hit the back foot of Achilles. Long ago, his mother had held on to that heel when she dipped her son into the magic river. His heel never touched the water. It was mortal, his weak spot.**

"Oh, man," said Josh. "Achilles died fighting in Troy."

"With an arrow in his heel," said Jess. "Just like the ancient stories said."

"Look," said Josh. He pointed below. Uncle Harry had taken the metal jar from Helen.

"What's he doing?" asked Jess, turning to Josh.

Josh glanced over the railing, watching his uncle. "He's hiding the jewels in the secret place."

Across the room, Paris ran toward Helen.

Just then King Menelaus and a small group of soldiers burst into the room.

Menelaus and Paris drew their weapons. The sounds of clashing swords filled the air. Helen was weeping. So many dead. So much sadness.

Uncle Harry raised his head from behind the statue of Athena.

"Come on," he called up to the twins. Then he rubbed his hands along the wall behind the statue.

No one noticed as Josh and Jess crawled down the stairs. Slowly they made their way to Uncle Harry.

"Hurry," said their uncle. He was looking for something on the wall.

Jess looked around. There was loud shouting from outside. More Greek soldiers were attacking the palace.

"What now?" asked Josh. They needed a plan to escape.

"We get out of here," said Uncle Harry.

Suddenly, he felt a lever in the wall. When he pressed it, a small door opened between two statues.

"This way," said Uncle Harry, waving to the twins.

Jess was the first to slip into the hidden passage. Josh and Uncle Harry followed. They walked for a long time. The dark tunnel twisted and turned under the city streets. They lit torches to show the way.

Jess stumbled on the rough stone path. "Be careful," said Josh, grabbing his sister before she fell.

"Yuck, spiders," said Jess. She ducked her head. Cobwebs hung from the low ceiling.

Finally, Uncle Harry stopped. He pushed against a small wooden door and stepped outside. Jess and Josh followed.

"We're safe," said Jess. The city walls were behind them. Jess coughed. Black smoke was in the air.

Josh looked up. Flames came out of the roofs of buildings.

"Troy is burning," he said. The Greeks had set fire to the city.

Everywhere they looked, Trojans tried to run. But they could not escape the enemy soldiers. The Greeks tied the hands of Trojans with heavy ropes. They were taking them back to Greece as slaves.

Uncle Harry pulled the twins away from the fighting. He lifted the leather bag from Josh's shoulder. Their uncle took out the time-compass and started to set the dials.

"It's over," he said. "Ten years of fighting."

Jess turned on the Wizard. She read aloud:



**The Trojan Horse helped the Greeks win the war. Paris was killed in the final battle and Troy was burned to the ground. King Menelaus sailed away with his army. He took Helen back to Greece.**

"Can we go home now?" asked Jess. Their mission was done.

"Yeah," said Josh. "The jewels are safe." They were buried in the ruins of Troy. Just as they were supposed to be.

Uncle Harry looked up. "Just one stop to

make," he said with a smile. The time-compass was clicking.

Josh and Jess looked at each other. They said together . . .

"Time-jump!"

## Chapter 10

# Detour to Delphi

"Where are we?" asked Jess. The sun was bright.

"Oh, man," said Josh, blinking. He was wearing Greek clothes. So were Jess and Uncle Harry.

The hillside was rocky. Olive trees grew along the side of the road. The time-compass had taken them to a new place.

"Delphi," said Uncle Harry. He pointed to the city on the hill.

"Are we still in ancient Greece?" asked Josh, looking around.

"Yes," said Uncle Harry. "But many years after the Trojan War."

Jess raised her hand and blocked the hot

sun. She gazed at the city up ahead. "Are we going there?" she asked.

Uncle Harry nodded. "Delphi is a sacred city. Many people visit the oracle." He pointed to the temple on the hill.

"What's an oracle?" asked Josh.

"A priestess who can predict the future. The ancient Greeks believe she speaks for the gods," said Uncle Harry.

Jess sat on a rock. "Oh, brother," she said. A pebble was in her sandal.

"Come on," said their uncle, heading toward the road.

Josh took off after Uncle Harry.

"Hey," said Jess, shaking out her sandal, "wait for me."

Jess caught up with Josh and Uncle Harry as they entered the city gates. The street opened up to a wide space with rows of stalls. People were selling food, clothes, and household goods. Busy shoppers filled the marketplace.

Jess sat down behind a stall and pulled out the Wizard. She read:

o wizard

The **agora** (AHG-ur-uh) was the center of a Greek town. It was the place to shop and to visit with friends. Public buildings and temples were located around the agora.

Jess looked through the crowd for Josh. She saw him, alone. He walked over.

"We're in the agora," said Jess, showing Josh the Wizard screen.

Jess looked around. "Where's Uncle Harry?"

"There," said Josh, "at the temple of Apollo." He pointed to the building at the top of the hill. "He said to wait here."

Jess frowned. What was her uncle up to now?

Josh sat down beside his sister. "And he said to stay out of trouble."

"What's so special about that temple?" wondered Jess. She typed some words, clicked, and read aloud:

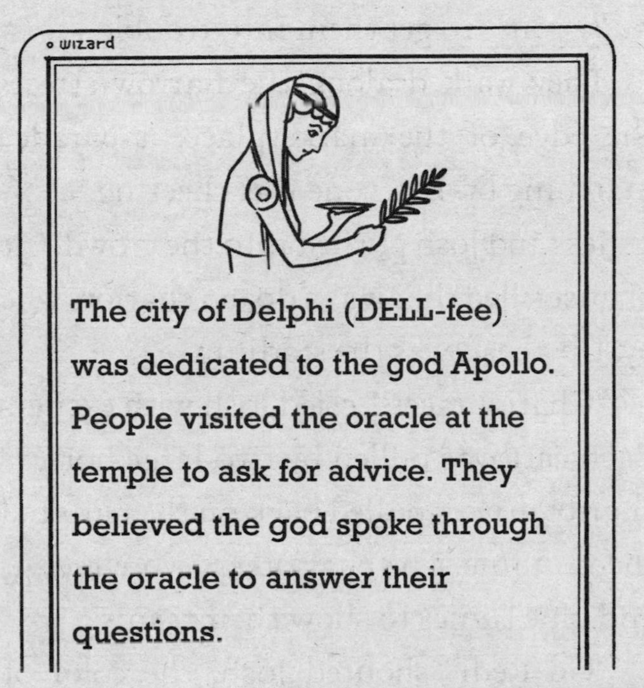


Josh shrugged. "Maybe Uncle Harry is seeing the oracle." He stretched and leaned back. Then he closed his eyes.

Jess stood up. She looked at Josh and frowned.

"Well, let's find out," said Jess, pulling her sleepy brother to his feet.

"Oh, man," said Josh. This time Jess was *really* going to get them into trouble.

They walked along the narrow streets. At the edge of the marketplace, a parade was marching by. Everyone was cheering.

Jess and Josh pushed into the crowd. Clouds of dust filled the air as a dozen chariots wheeled by. Up ahead was the stadium.

"Chariot races!" cried Josh with excitement. Each cart was pulled by two large horses. The chariot drivers pulled back on the reins to keep them in line. The charioteers wore red, green, and blue tunics to show their teams.

"Go Red!" shouted Josh, the color of his favorite Boston team. The charioteer with the red tunic turned and nodded. Josh waved back. He remembered Achilles and the wild chariot ride to Troy.

"Oh, no," said Jess. "Don't even think about it!"

There was no time to go to the races. Jess grabbed her brother's arm and led him toward the temple.

"Hey," said Josh, watching the chariots turn the corner.

"Come on," she said. "We have to find Uncle Harry."

Josh glanced back at the stadium. He wondered which charioteer would win the race.

A few minutes later, Jess and Josh rushed up the steps to the temple. A huge statue of the god Apollo stood at the entrance, casting a large shadow on the wall. It was quiet. Too quiet.

"It's creepy here," said Jess. Her voice made an echo. In front of them was a large round room with a high ceiling. Tall columns held up the marble roof. Scenes of Greek gods and heroes were carved into the stone.

"Hurry," said Josh. They took off down the hall. Their footsteps echoed on the tile floor.

"Try to be quiet," warned Jess. Voices were coming from the center of the round room.

Josh looked around. "Over here," he whispered. They ducked behind a column.

Something was strange.

When Jess looked up, she saw Uncle Harry. He was sitting on a three-legged stool in the middle of the room. He was alone, staring into a large hole in the floor.

And talking.

## Chapter 11
# The Oracle

Jess and Josh stood still for a long time. They watched Uncle Harry from their hiding place.

Josh looked around. He was puzzled.

"There's no one here," he said. "Who is Uncle Harry talking to?"

"The oracle," whispered Jess. A chill ran down her spine.

Josh stared at the hole in the middle of the floor. *Did Uncle Harry believe the ancient stories?*

Jess felt in her pocket for the Wizard. She typed in some words. The twins put their heads together over the screen and read:

wizard

**The temple of Apollo was built over a crack in the earth where gas escapes. The priestess, or oracle, went down to the temple basement. Some scientists believed she breathed in this gas and then answered questions. The vapors from the gas put her into a trance.**

"The oracle isn't real," said Jess. "It's a trick."

"Yeah, no magic," said Josh. "Just gas from the earth."

Jess nodded. "I guess that's where the oracle gets her power."

"So the ancient Greeks believed," said Josh.

They watched as their uncle leaned over the hole. He said something to the oracle. A voice echoed from below.

Josh shook his head. "I still don't get it."

"What do you mean?" asked Jess.

"Uncle Harry must know the trick," said Josh.

"Maybe he's not asking for advice," whispered Jess.

Their uncle took the leather bag from his shoulder. Then he reached into the hole.

"What's he doing?" asked Josh. Something was in Uncle Harry's hand. Something the oracle had given him.

Uncle Harry opened the leather bag. Carefully, he put the thing inside.

"She's the one," said Jess with a knowing smile. "I bet she gives him the lost objects!"

"Like the wax book from Pompeii, and the statues from Tut's mask," said Josh slowly.

Jess gazed at her Uncle. "And Helen's gold jewels." She remembered all the sacred objects from their time travels with Uncle Harry.

"What about the time-compass?" said Josh. It was magic from the time-compass that took them into the past.

Jess nodded. Now that *was* a mystery.

Suddenly, Uncle Harry sat up and put the leather bag on his shoulder. He turned his head and said some final words to the oracle.

Jess tugged on the sleeve of Josh's tunic. "Maybe we should leave," she said quietly.

"Right," said Josh. "Before Uncle Harry sees us."

Hand in hand, they hurried out of the temple. They walked the city streets until they found the agora.

"There!" shouted Josh, pointing to the meeting place near the stall. He ran down the paved street. Jess took after him, careful not to fall. Then he pulled her down to the ground.

They sat there, out of breath.

Jess was the first to speak. "What do we do?"

Josh shrugged. "We keep Uncle Harry's secret. All of it. The time-compass, the sacred objects . . ."

". . . and the oracle," Jess added.

Josh nodded. He thought about their time travels with Uncle Harry.

"I wonder what the oracle gave him this time," said Josh. He was ready for another adventure.

"Whatever it is," said Jess, "one thing we know for sure . . ."

"What's that?" said Josh.

Jess looked determined. She forgot her fears. "Uncle Harry will need our help."

Down the street between the stalls, the twins saw a familiar shape.

Uncle Harry was back.

## Chapter 12

# Home Again

"Uncle Harry!" cried Jess.

"We're here!" shouted Josh, rushing to meet their uncle.

Uncle Harry smiled. "Hungry?" he asked, glancing around. The smell of warm bread drifted in from the next stall.

Two small heads nodded.

"How about a burger!" said Josh, rubbing his belly.

"Yeah," said Jess. "With pickles!"

Uncle Harry laughed. He led the twins toward a wooden table with three small stools.

"Wait here," he said, walking over to the owner of the stall.

A large piece of meat was roasting on a spit over the fire. Juices were dripping down into the flames. The owner cut off slices. He put the meat on a thin bread and folded it in half, making sandwiches. Uncle Harry brought them to the table.

Josh carried a clay bowl of goat cheese, octopus, and olives. Jess filled a jar with water. They sat down.

"Lunch," said Uncle Harry. They grabbed sandwiches and ate quickly.

Jess tried some of the cheese. "Mmm," she said. "This is good."

"Better than the octopus?" asked Josh, grinning.

Jess made a face. "No, thanks," she said. "I had some at the Greek camp. Remember?"

Josh looked at Jess. The huge wooden horse. The battles. Briseis and Achilles. All a memory now.

Jess turned to her uncle. “Can we go home?” she asked.

Silently, Uncle Harry stood up. The twins followed. They hurried through the streets and out the city gate. They stopped at an empty spot in the olive grove.

Uncle Harry reached into his leather bag. He pulled out the time-compass.

“Will you come with us?” asked Josh. He watched his uncle set the hands on the device.

"Not this time," said their uncle, shaking his head. "I have more work to do."

"Here?" asked Jess. "In ancient Greece?"

Uncle Harry looked around. "No," he said. "Somewhere very different." He was lost in his thoughts.

Josh was worried. "But you'll need our help."

"Will you send for us?" asked Jess.

Uncle Harry nodded. "You guys are awesome!" he said and smiled.

Jess and Josh looked at each other. They didn't want to say good-bye.

"Stand back," said their uncle, turning the hands of the time-compass one last time. The familiar clicking sound grew louder and louder.

Josh grabbed Jess's hand as a blast of light cut across the sky. The wind blew through the trees. Then it was still.

Jess looked up.

They were back in the attic.

* * *

Josh looked out the window of the Boston house. Snowflakes were falling. No time had passed since they left for Troy.

"It's really coming down," said Josh, pointing to the snow.

Jess was sitting on the old trunk. The Wizard was in her hand.

"Yeah," said Jess. She typed in D-E-L-P-H-I and pressed the Search button.

Josh walked over.

"Look at this," she said. Josh leaned over the Wizard's screen.

"My guy won!" yelled Josh. He stared at the face of the red-team charioteer.

Jess looked at Josh. "It's not real, you know. All these stories."

"Maybe not the oracle," said Josh. "But Troy was a real city."

They glanced at the old trunk. It was covered with stickers from all over the world.

"Where will Uncle Harry go next?" asked Jess.

Josh shrugged. "No clues this time."

"We'll just have to wait until he needs our help," said Jess. The trapdoor to the attic was open.

Josh grabbed the flashlight and led the way down the ladder. Jess was right behind him.

"Come on," Josh said. "Let's go build a snowman!"